The Careless Hedgehogs

and The Little Clockwinder

illustrated by
Gary Rees

AWARD PUBLICATIONS LIMITED

The Careless Hedgehogs

Once upon a time, Hoo, the owl, found a baby elf cuddled up in his nest.

'Tu-whit!' he said, most astonished. 'Who are you?' The baby elf stared at him, but didn't answer a word.

Hoo perched on the side of his nest, and wondered what he should do with the strange little creature.

'I'll go and ask my friend Prickles,' he said at last. 'He is wise, and will tell me.'

Off he flew.

Prickles, the hedgehog, was awake, just outside his house.

'Good evening,' said Hoo politely.

'Good evening,' answered Prickles. 'Why have you come to see me?'

'In my nest there is a strange little elf creature that will not speak a word,' explained Hoo. 'What am I to do with it?'

'A little elf thing!' said Prickles, sitting up quickly. 'What is it like?'

'It is small, with coloured wings,' answered Hoo.

'Have you seen the notice the King of Fairyland has put up everywhere?' asked Prickles excitedly.

'No,' said Hoo.

'Come and I'll show it to you,' said Prickles, scuttling off.

Presently they came to a tall foxglove.
Hanging on it was a notice which said:

LOST FROM DREAMLAND

LITTLE ELF BABY WITH COLOURED
WINGS. ANYONE FINDING IT
SHALL HAVE A GREAT REWARD.
PLEASE TELL THE
KING OF FAIRYLAND.

'There!' said Prickles. 'You must have found the lost baby elf.'

'But how could it have got into my nest?' asked Hoo, very puzzled.

'Don't bother about *that*!' answered Prickles. 'Go and tell the King you've found it!'

THE CARELESS HEDGEHOGS

'Will you take care of it while I'm gone?' asked Hoo.

'Yes,' said Prickles. 'I'll get all the fairy hedgehogs I know to look after it.'

So Hoo flew down to the hedgehogs, carrying the elf baby carefully.

'Now look after it carefully,' he said, flying off to the King's palace.

THE CARELESS HEDGEHOGS

All the fairy hedgehogs sat down in a ring, and looked at the baby. It lay in the middle of them and laughed and kicked.

'I think perhaps the bad gnomes stole it,' said Prickles. 'They are enemies to the people of Dreamland.'

Whenever any one came near the little baby, the hedgehogs stiffened all their prickles, and made the very worst noise they could.

'Here comes Hoo!' cried Prickles at last. Hoo perched on the tree above him.

'It *is* the lost baby,' he cried, 'and the King of Dreamland is coming to fetch it in two days. The King says you must take great care of it till then, and give it honey to eat and dew to drink.'

'Very well,' said Prickles.

'And,' said Hoo flying off, 'you must see that the bad gnomes don't come for it again.'

So all that day the hedgehogs watched the elf baby. Prickles fetched it honey from the heather and dew from the grasses. All through the night the fairy hedgehogs watched, and the next day Prickles said, 'I'm going to fetch a special dew from the red blackberry leaves. Be very careful while I am gone.'

Off he went.

Then one of the little hedgehogs stretched itself.

'I'm *so* tired of watching,' he said, 'I'm going off for a little walk.'

He ran off through the grass, but in a minute he came back looking very excited.

'Come quickly!' he cried. 'There is a fairy dance by the foxgloves tonight, and if we're quick we can all go and hear the music.'

The hedgehogs thought that would be lovely.

'We'll go to the dance till Prickles comes back!' they cried. 'He'll never know.'

Off they scampered as fast as they could, and were soon having a glorious time.

The little elf baby, finding there was nobody to stop it, crawled away by itself, and fell fast asleep under a mushroom a little way off.

Suddenly there was a great fluttering of wings, and down flew the King of Dreamland and the King of Fairyland; they had come to fetch the lost elf baby. At the same moment up came Prickles too, with his blackberry dew for the baby.

'Where is the baby?' cried the King of Dreamland.

'I don't know,' answered Prickles, looking astonished. 'It was here when I left, guarded by lots of fairy hedgehogs. Now they're all gone!'

At that moment, back came the hedgehogs from the dance. They looked very frightened when they saw that the baby was gone and the two Kings had come.

'How *dare* you disobey my orders?' said the King of Fairyland to the trembling hedgehogs.

THE CARELESS HEDGEHOGS

'Please, we're very sorry,' said the hedgehogs.

'That doesn't help matters,' the King of Dreamland said angrily. 'Now the baby has gone again, and perhaps the bad gnomes have stolen it away just because you weren't watching!'

THE CARELESS HEDGEHOGS

'I shall have to punish you,' said the Fairy King, 'You haven't been good hedgehogs, so perhaps you will be good if I change you into something else!'

He waved his hand. In a minute all the fairy hedgehogs found themselves climbing up a big chestnut tree.

The King waved his wand again.

The hedgehogs climbed along the branches, turned green, and sat quite still.

'There!' said the King. 'Now perhaps they will keep the baby chestnuts from harm until they're ripe. Now, Prickles, hunt around until you find the elf baby.'

THE CARELESS HEDGEHOGS

Of course Prickles found him under the mushroom very quickly, and brought him back to the King of Dreamland.

But Prickles is very lonely now without the other hedgehogs. They never come down to play with him, because they are so busy looking after the baby chestnuts, and they are much more careful of them than they were of the little elf baby.

THE CARELESS HEDGEHOGS

And if you look at a chestnut tree in October, you'll see what the King changed the hedgehogs into – and you'll find they're still very prickly!

The Little Clockwinder

Dickory Dock was the clockwinder to the king of Elfland. The King was very fond of clocks and he had a great many. He liked them all to show the same time, and to strike and chime exactly at the right minute. Dickory Dock was supposed to wind them each night – but, you know, he often didn't, and then the clocks went wrong.

One day the King gave him a magic key. 'Look, Dickory Dock,' he said, 'here is an enchanted key that will wind up anything in the world, no matter what it is – but you, of course, must simply use it for clocks. Instead of keeping a hundred different keys, as you have always had to do, you may now throw them all away and use just this one for every clock in the palace.'

THE LITTLE CLOCKWINDER

Dickory Dock was delighted – but, even though his work was now much easier, he didn't always remember to wind up the clocks.

One day the King was so cross that he spanked Dickory Dock hard with his best blue slipper. Then wasn't Dickory Dock in a temper!

How he vowed he would punish the King for spanking him! What a lot of rubbish he talked – and in the end, he thought of the naughtiest, silliest idea imaginable.

'I'll use my magic key and wind up everything in the palace!' he cried.

Straight away he began to do this. He
wound up every chair, big and small,
every table, round or square, every stool
and every bookcase. He even wound up
the books, the vases and the cushions –
and when the King and Queen came
home that night, what a strange and
mysterious sight met their eyes!

'Bless us all!' cried the Queen, as a
table came dancing up to her. 'What's
this?'

'Mercy on us!' shouted the King, as two chairs ran up to him and danced round him. 'What's happened?'

'Look at that stool!' cried the Queen. 'It's dancing with my best red cushion! Everything's alive!'

THE LITTLE CLOCKWINDER

'Dickory Dock has been using the magic key I gave him!' stormed the King in a rage. 'Get away, you clumsy great table, you're treading on my toe. Just look at those books rushing round the room! Where's Dickory Dock? Fetch him at once!'

THE LITTLE CLOCKWINDER

Dickory Dock was hiding behind the door.

THE LITTLE CLOCKWINDER

A footman peeped into the room when he heard the King shouting, and in a second he caught the mischievous clock-winder by the shoulder, and brought him before the King. Two or three cups came and ran round them, and a saucer rolled all the way up the stately footman's leg. It was really most peculiar.

'Go away from Elfland at once!' roared
the King in a fury. 'Never come back!
Give me your key, and I'll wind you up so
you'll have to keep on walking and never
stop. That will be a good punishment for
you!' With that he dug the magic key into
the frightened elf and wound him up.

THE LITTLE CLOCKWINDER

Poor Dickory Dock! He started running off and it wasn't long before he came to our land. He has been here ever since. What do you suppose he does? He winds up the dandelion clocks, of course! He's just as careless over those as he used to be over the clocks in the palace, and that is why they are so seldom right! Puff one and see!

For further information on Enid Blyton please contact www.blyton.com

ISBN 0-86163-720-8

Text copyright The Enid Blyton Company
Illustrations copyright © 1994 Award Publications Limited

Enid Blyton's signature is a trademark of The Enid Blyton Company

The Careless Hedgehogs first published in *Pinkity's Pranks
and Other Nature Fairy Tales*
The Little Clockwinder first published in *Book of the Year*

This edition first published 1998 by Award Publications Limited,
27 Longford Street, London NW1 3DZ

Printed in India